Tweenies™

What big eyes you have, Grandma!

BBC

One day, Max told the Tweenies the story of Little Red Riding Hood. The Tweenies enjoyed it so much they decided to do a play.

"I'll be Little Red Riding Hood," said Bella. "Fizz can be my mummy and Milo can be my daddy."

"Who can I be?" asked Jake.

"You can be my grandma," Bella told him.

"No!" cried Jake. "I want to be the WOLF!"

Fizz thought he was too small to be the wolf, but Jake said that if he couldn't be the wolf he wouldn't be in the play AT ALL! So Max said he would be Grandma and Judy would tell the story.

The Tweenies rummaged through the dressing-up box for costumes. Fizz found a net curtain to wrap around herself. Jake found a fluffy scarf for a tail and made a cardboard wolf nose. Milo dressed up in a cap and coat.

"I can't find anything RED to wear!" cried Bella.

Milo suggested that she wore a blue dress, which made Bella very cross.

"I'm Little RED Riding Hood," she told him. "Not Little BLUE Riding Hood!"

Luckily, Max found a piece of red curtain that was just right for a hood and cloak.

When Judy put some real cakes in Little Red Riding Hood's basket, Jake wanted to eat one straightaway.

"Not now, Jake," said Judy. "We're about to start our play."

Judy began. Once upon a time, there was a little girl called Little Red Riding Hood.

"Hello," said Bella. "I am Little Red Riding Hood and this lady is my mummy."

"Hello," said Fizz.

Little Red Riding Hood's daddy, who'd been chopping wood in the forest, walked into the cottage.

"Hello," said Milo.

"This feather duster is my pretend axe, because real axes are dangerous."

Little Red Riding Hood's mummy wanted her to take a basket of cakes to Grandma, who was poorly and lived all alone in a little cottage in the forest.

"DON'T talk to anyone on the way," said Daddy.

"OK," said Little Red Riding Hood.

"I won't be long." And off she skipped.

"You've forgotten the basket," Mummy called after her.

"Oops," giggled Little Red Riding Hood. "Sorry!"

Little Red Riding Hood set off again and soon she met a wicked wolf.

"Hello," growled Jake. "I'm a friendly, big, bad, hungry, wicked wolf. Can I have one of those cakes in your basket?"

"No, you can't," said Little Red Riding Hood. "I'm taking them to my grandma who is poorly and lives all alone in a little cottage in the forest."

The wicked wolf grinned and ran off to find Grandma's house.

Grandma was in bed, waiting for Little Red Riding Hood. Then,

KNOCK KNOCK!

"Is that you, Little Red Riding Hood?" called Max, in a special, grandma voice.

"Yes," squeaked the wolf. "I've brought you a basket of cakes."

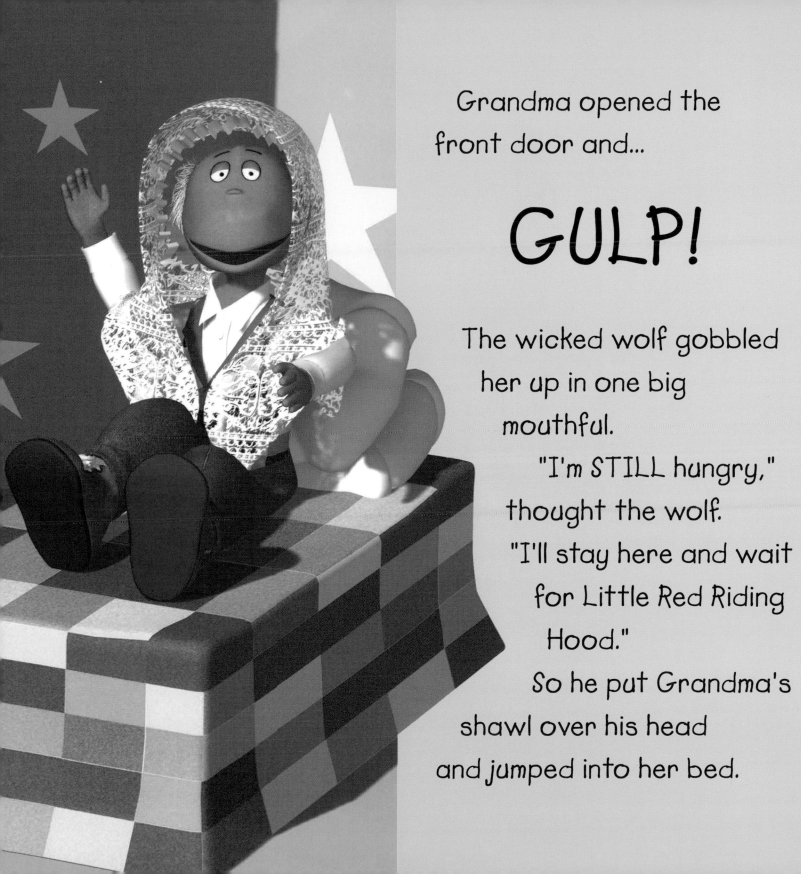

Grandma opened the front door and...

GULP!

The wicked wolf gobbled her up in one big mouthful.

"I'm STILL hungry," thought the wolf. "I'll stay here and wait for Little Red Riding Hood."

So he put Grandma's shawl over his head and jumped into her bed.

A few minutes later, Little Red Riding Hood knocked on the door.

KNOCK KNOCK!

"Come in, my dear," squeaked the wolf.

Little Red Riding Hood STARED at her grandma.

"You're looking very furry," she said. "And what BIG EARS you have, Grandma!"

Jake couldn't remember what to say next, so Bella said it for him. "All the better to hear you with!"

"What BIG EYES you have, Grandma," cried Little Red Riding Hood.

"All the better to eat you with," squeaked the wicked wolf.

"It's not 'eat'," whispered Bella. "You SEE with your eyes!"

"Sorry," giggled Jake. "All the better to SEE you with!"

"What BIG TEETH you have, Grandma!"
cried Little Red Riding Hood.
"HAH! All the better to EAT you with!"
growled the wicked wolf, and
jumped out of bed.

Then...

GULP!

He gobbled
her up, too!

"I'm STILL hungry," said the wolf. "I think I'll try a cake."

Just then, Little Red Riding Hood's mummy and daddy ran into the cottage.

"Not so fast, you wicked wolf!" cried Daddy. "I saw what you did to Little Red Riding Hood. Take that!" He whacked the wolf with his feather duster, chased him into the forest and turned him upside down.

Out popped Grandma
and Little Red Riding Hood!

"Mummy, we've been saved!" cried Little Red Riding Hood.
"You and Grandma must say 'thank you' to Daddy for
rescuing you," said Mummy. "Here he comes now."
Daddy said he'd chased the wolf out of the forest, across
the land, up a mountain and ALL the way to the moon!

"Well, we certainly won't be seeing that wicked wolf again!" said Grandma. "Now, let's eat those delicious cakes."

"So they all lived happily ever after," said Judy. "The end."

But then...

KNOCK KNOCK!

"Who can that be?" asked Grandma.

It was the wicked wolf! "I'm STILL hungry,"
he said. "Can I have a cake now?"

THE real END